Lucy Blackman

Talking of Macbeth:

Short Fiction by the author of
Lucy's Story:
Autism and other Adventures.

Lucy Blackman Books
Brisbane Australia

First published by,
Book in Hand, Brisbane, Australia 2009
ISBN 978-0-9806033-0-9
Book in Hand at Smashwords 2013

This edition
Lucy Blackman Books
978-0-9756345-2-3

Table of Contents

Author's note

I have never spoken fluently and I was nearly fifteen years old before I could write down some of the thoughts which floated in my brain. My hearing was so weird that I found language spoken by others a meaningless blur.

If you want to meet the person that I am, read *Flat Reflections in the Round* and *Dragons of Bass Strait*.

Then in 1992, when I was nineteen, my hearing changed a little bit. For the first time, I could distinguish regional accents. I discovered this sitting at Los Angeles International Airport waiting to fly home to Australia. A year later the news of rape camps in the former Yugoslavia hit the news, and these two events form the basis of *Miriam*.

I had learnt to write stories in which speech is a building block for narrative.

Miriam (1993)

Outside the sweating layered portholes Melbourne rose. Smooth and black, black rain on runways, black roads on suburbs to be reached, the light on the runway fragmented by the rain – sparkles that shaded in her tired mind to the glittering glowing of Darrell Lea shops, Melbourne's glimpse of magic, full of chocolate and licorice in silver and gold, floodlit and in her mind still outshining the imported yellow arches and red, white and blue jeans shops with which they were cloistered in concrete.

Each shopping centre turned inwards from the curtained homogenous population, safe behind windows where the Box contained the lantern show of royal marital disaster, and economic doom, and Bosnia flashing under the stripped fuselage of relief flights dropping the means of life heaven knew where.

The airport at Los Angeles had been different. Different from Melbourne, and different from being in an airport with her father. Marie and the fat man had sat side by side in vinyl and chrome chairs unaware that their twinning was to span the Pacific and then south.

Behind her Marie could hear Australia Abroad – beery male slurry voice saying,

"Mohammed, shut up. Girlie, for christ's sake keep your brother quiet!"

Three bodies slumping tiredly into chairs siameselike twinned in the same chrome frame. The blonde boy in the Collingwood jumper, looking out of the windows at the kaleidoscope of landing lights and flashing beacons on moving planes lashing tired eyes. He lifted his imaginary gun, and intoned the traditional 'bang-bang' interspersed with the most extraordinary wailing.

The same male voice growled again and the adolescent Australian female voice said, "For goodness sake, he isn't doing any harm!" – a stranger's voice more familiar to Marie than her own, the voice of young Edna E.

Mid-Pacific, Marie sat between her own disposable antimacassar and that which stuck crookedly to the seat in front of her. Shit, LA seemed a lifetime ago. Her father had been so urgent and excited when he and that woman with the smooth suit and that film-star-face had left her there.

Now she was suddenly dreadfully frightened, and that was something that she did not remember ever being before, not to the extent that her diaphragm hurt and her eyes glazed. This lonely homecoming possibly might be the end of her happy and confident world, an open ended shute that would catapult Marie-that-she-knew into the life of Marie-who-she-did-not-know – the Marie who did not go to the same school as her mother and her father's sister, the school where the regulation and expensive clothes were ritually updated at the beginning of each school season regardless of the realities of climate change in the real world.

That unknown world was where Mary was now, and Marie could not conceptualise such a migration. Did one stay the same when other things changed? Would she still be Marie if she did not have regular stylish cuts that left her hair chocolate-smooth and sharply angular against the neck as did the majority of the Year Nine kids that she hung about with?

Shit! That was a joke. She didn't 'hang-about' except in school hours when there was an unoccupied lunchtime. That was not what hanging-about was. Hanging-about was what Mary was doing when she had seen her, flashing by, from the express train. She, Marie, had been sitting quite still and the station had swept past but photographed forever. Mary turning to light something in her mouth from the man in a bike jacket. Definitely a man, not a boy! Marie knew it was to avoid this world that her mother ferried her in the glossy station wagon on most convenient occasions.

Did hair make a difference? Would having hair like an unravelled rope, with a topknot held in a kind of twisted pink rosette, make the person underneath different? The Scrunchie that collected the tow-like strands of the girl over the aisle – the same girl she had heard at Los Angeles and watched on the flight talk to and mother both the big blonde man who had solidly sunk beer after beer round a third of the globe and the little boy who sat between her and the window. Was it a certain kind of person who wore a Scrunchie like that, or was it the hair that shaped the person?

Then was the slob who sat right beside her, Marie, different from how he would be if he were thin? He wasn't very nice anyway. He was gross. She played with the word with pleasure. Before she had been transformed, Mary had called down a strong rebuke from a dedicated English teacher for calling the death scene in Hamlet GROSS.

As the plane started its slow descent, the novelty of double meaning entranced Marie while watching a thigh-thick sausage vibrating slightly on the shared arm of their seats. A hand at the end was waving flacidly to some unknown sound through the headphones. The stolid face sank into multiple rolls of fat that became a mound of stretched T-shirt that abruptly turned to swollen denim and terminated in two tubby feet that were stuffed into airline sockettes.

Marie blinked back tears and got a crazy idea that she was reading her own reactions in a 'Sweet Dreams' book. The stewardess dropped the Customs Declarations forms for completion onto the outlaid trays, and smiled sweetly across Marie.

"If this girl has problems filling this in, can you give her a hand, Sir?"

The polite Americanised response did not make Marie any less determined to not address a word to him. His lack of interest in her international travels in the first minutes of the crossing had frozen her comments on her American flight in her throat.

She completed her mixture of ticks and signatures and glanced at the girl with the hair. The father was snoring noisily and Blondie was looking at the form as if it would bite. For the second or third time the stewardess stopped and smiled at the little boy, and bent her own head towards the girl, pointing to boxes and lines for the borrowed pen to rest on. Together they puzzled over the immigration form and the pair of passports. The stewardess laboriously transcribed a collection of consonants and assorted vowels from the page which carried the picture of a broad-faced woman with her hair tucked under a scarf, and the portraits of the two children alongside the Australian coat of arms.

Marie turned to find her own card being scrutinised by a pair of porky eyes. "So you can read and write, huh! Not bad. That's mine. Don't worry, fair's fair. I don't mind you seeing mine."

She could hardly avoid seeing the sheet thrust at her – work permit granted: Teacher. This poor man probably was not so bad, just seriously revolting. This was the moment she missed her father more than ever. Not that he was so close but he was never embarrassing and always reliable when he was there. This might have been the way it as with Mary. Had she known things were going to change? The poor kid, living in a crummy flat with her mum! A friend had been there, and the friend had said that the father skipped and married in Europe. No maintenance. The topic of maintenance and access was a hot one at school.

The cluster of organisms that had first fused together above the swirling lights of the Californian coast began to decompose. As the passengers prepared to land, the girl across the aisle nudged her dad.

The girls both started to move towards the toilet. For the first time the little boy did not move. He sat in his seat rigid with exhaustion. Marie spoke over her shoulder.

"Did you like the States? Cool, huh?"

"Didn't see 'em, came straight through from Europe to get home quick," and turned slowly to look firmly out of a window.

"See your mum stayed behind?"

"Mind your own bloody business!"

And when Marie came out of the cubicle she could see the long hair dropping onto the fashion pages of the glossy in-flight magazine.

Before Fatso returned from the loo, Marie slipped into her seat and glared possessively at the electric jewels rising beneath them.

At the terminal two women stood chatting politely. The teacher thought about the six months' exchange in a Los Angeles school. At least the Academy would not have gun-toting students. She wanted to meet her replacement and make him feel at home. It was nice that A Mother was there. It would give the new arrival a reassurance as to the kind of families whose daughters he would be teaching.

The other woman babbled into the vacuum ... Marie's maturity and understanding ... and how relieved her husband had been to sign the contract that would save the firm ... and how two trips to the airport in three days was such a bind ... and wasn't it nice the way the ethnics always brought so many people ...

The teacher had moved. Brittle and bleached under the fluorescent light she held out a hand to an enormously fat man in motor cycle boots.

The mother was surrounded now by foreign voices, foreign in a way that Greek and Italian were not then in Melbourne. The strange group behind swept forward, the men stockily grim with hands outstretched and their women in long sleeves and knotted headscarves celebrating the homecoming of one of their own. The door behind the barrier slid open.

Flat Reflections in the Round (1992)

Someone like me must be very mysterious to anyone outside the barrier. Smashing that barrier is only possible in the mind, and that is where stories are born.

So once upon a family...

Now I sit here, lost in a city which I have reached by chance. The only familiar thing is the Big Mac container on the table and the typewriter beside the motel tariffs. Later people will fetch me, but for the moment I must remember light and sound and warmth in the good world of first awareness. The person I am was once a child, and surely I can see it through the eyes of a child like me.

Nappies on the hoist whirled against the blue sky, carrying hopes and flashes of fear and delight. The lines were parallel yet circular streaks and angles cut the space that cried to the eye as a void that was also a containment. Round and round and round again. The fat white cloud came to break the sky and her safety started to go as nappies and cloud and single strangling silver wires melded and flew. The voice called and saved her, but she did not turn. Hands from behind gripped firmly, carrying the sensitive body to the other part of her world where her ears and eyes registered safety and the wildness of existence was bearable.

Are you starting to see the image as the child saw it? The way that the other person is not developed outside her senses is full of the impression that I want to give. That is not because that is how I remember my childhood, but it encapsulates some of the sensations that made the safe world in which I lived.

The dishes were on the firm surface of the table, and the unyielding wood caught the shock of the metallic crash of the spoon swirling downwards in the chubby hand. Unlike the others at the table, she felt the food with her other hand, testing the texture then dipping her face to sniff it before the spoon came across and dexterously shovelled to her mouth. The chair swung back and the man at the head of the table reached out to catch the back as the child compensated with a forward shift. It rested as a feather on her father's hand as the legs balanced the curve of her body in the acrobatic seesaw of a circus act.

I am learning to see a difference in focus is almost unavoidable. This passage wrapped the child in the care of her family and the pleasure of her sensations, and is probably nearer to the memories that I live with. Unlike her, I swung the chair in part for the reassurance of the roar of disapproval, but to show the apparent disassociation of this changeling her comprehension should seem slight.

Around her came her family's laughter and the pride of a ten year old voice. She could now link the words "climbed over the fence" with the scratchy flight to freedom that had been spurred by the noise of the kindergarten.

So there is the child's perspective again! I wonder if it is possible to write an entire short story so focussed on immediate attention. Probably not and, even there, there is a point of reference. The child's age and size fall into place in that word 'kindergarten'. The thoughts that the vision and sounds of my lost home bring are undermining the composition of this. There is no memory of such a conversation, and the family I have invented is not mine. Still that absorbed little girl is part of me, and the hurt is sharpening this knife edge of memory.

Around her the words whirled and ebbed, and the thoughts of her people were thrown around the stillness of her face. The words the child heard meant little, but the hurt came from the man's tone and the feeling of loudness that was somehow concerned with her. Some words made pictures of people or places. "Hearing" meant the place of terror where her mother's hand held big things on her ears and she had had to scream to keep the noise out. There was a word that meant blocks and pictures that she was meant to do something with, and having her screaming talked about. Her big people had been very upset that day. The next words sounded like "hands" but had something to do with the man in the chair with the big wheels who was pushed past the front gate in the mornings. This was a word that was said a lot in the next few minutes.

The challenge of the food absorbed her again, and the peanut butter jar started to take on an obsessional importance as a longing for the texture and taste washed all else from her mind. Her hands and face smeared with brown, and the short hair became spiked with the same colour. An aroma of peanut engulfed the family.

The water hurtled from the tap to hit the white enamel. Experienced palms grabbing the wriggling body around the ribs were careful to be firm and very heavy in touch. The soft water lapped against the edge of the bath, and under the water the appearance of the legs distorted. Screaming, the struggling child passed from anguish to blind terror. The towel loomed and the rough threads stood out in serried shattering ranks.

At this point the character of the mother comes into focus very slightly. If the child sees her, the reader will not get the impression that the mother herself would have of her daughter. She would probably have thought, as my mother would have, that her own child did not react to her. So wrong, I know, to believe the child did not love, but to make the perspective of the child limited is a way of drawing a picture for the onlooker. And what did the screaming child I was, give to her?

The carpet-deadened patter of the footsteps as the spinning child careered through the house caught the attention of her father, but he drew back as the wail of pleasure started to drown out the radio. Newly fearless, his daughter gyrated through the house to fly above the world to the haven of the top bunk.

So, I used to scramble but to the pursuer the speed appeared magical. There my childhood-self sits as I did, happy and secure in close confining space. Can now bring the two most closely involved people in this story together. For a child to be loved is a need, but for this child also a terror. And I am still addressing the problem of bringing unnamed and faceless characters to life and allowing the reader to make a clear picture in his mind. Did I ever see my mother, or is it the photograph in my wallet that gives me a face to appear in this frame?

The mother's face appeared over the bunk-board, and then two tickling hands reached forward so that the girl reached the floor in a parabola of squeals and wriggles that melded happily into the dressing ritual. The two faces met in a wisp of a kiss before a stinging and tingling brought the smile to a spasm of distaste.

Now there is a problem of how to bring my character onto the stage of the larger world. It is outside her family that an answer to this mystery lies. They may know but the reader does not. Visualising her as not registering events in sequence, I have opted for the slide show approach, with each scene sweeping over the previous one, but here there is a break.

The woman groaned with mock resentment as her ankle twisted on the edge of the curb. The piggybacked burden did not grip, so she clasped her hands below her daughter's legs. That left a body that swung back and swayed to each movement, while the arms flailed purposelessly. As the pair moved to the wide space of the park a runner drew alongside. Relieved, the mother put the child down, but carefully retained a full grip on both wrists before handing an arm to her son. The hands starred outwards and did not clasp. There was no desire to cup another's hand, no revulsion but no urge.

As the pair moved towards the wide space of the park, the hands that held each wrist were relaxed. The mother and son laughed at the ecstasy they swung between them as they walked to the park, but the rough ground signalled a shift, and the body was lifted to a hip as high as her own head. Below swung denim legs and the travelling grass. Above her was the sky and beside her a woolly arm. The sleeve rubbed the cheek that rested on it. A scream split the mood and the clasp on the child tightened.

The swing moved, running on grooves of air. The rush and dip gave depth to the world and anxiety receded. The table on the ridge gave the gathered adults a panoramic view of the playground. A flurry of children moved around until none was distinguishable from the others. Sound and colour turned on the carousel until the call to move.

That was my real world, the world of stimulation and motion. This may be a fictional account but this view that I have is not fiction. This is the reality that is the present memory. Which is the truth, my happiness or the way the other world saw me?

Her legs drove towards the light at the further end of the avenue of tree-trunks. The gathering branches closed off the threat of unlimited sky. The voices at the playground died and swelled. After the brownish-green gloom, there was a bursting gleam of sun over the rough grass that curved to the line of power pylons. The headlong joyous scamper ended in still rapt contemplation of the straight soaring triangles linked by the parallel loops of buzzing wire that strung across the greenbelt. Under the angles, the child stood rapt and alone.

She rested her hand on the steel strut and turned. The horns before her held no fears. But below! The eyes, large and insistent, demanding she meet them if only for a moment. Eyes above an inquisitive warm muzzle. There was no escape but stillness. So she sat, soles of her feet pressed together and head turned sideways to shut out the vision she could not flee.

The policeman handed the small damp figure to her mother, who looked somehow at a loss as to what to do next. The screams started to rotate as threshing arms and legs fought for freedom. The vacant eyed man at the nearby barbecue jammed one hand in his ear and bit strongly on the heel of his other hand. The staring families around the playground absorbed the new spectacle. The older woman moved over from her adult son and placed a restraining hand on the almost free child. Over her head and through the fury of her restraint, the little girl heard the voice, "Well, that's autism for you!"

So that is the word, and even now the fear comes when I type it. A vision of a distortion of myself in a very shadowy fictional family. There, thinking of it, is a one dimensional aspect to this, but then I am one dimensional sometimes, aren't I?

Goldilocks and Son (1992)

As the girl paused at the door of the McDonalds a wave of eyes swept over her and withdrew. Her height gave her a clear view of the illuminated menu and the smaller mortals over whom she seemed to tower had an equally clear glimpse of her gilt hair. At a third glance one could see that it was not really gold. The spikes were pinky with a subdued sparkle, but the midwinter sun streaming through the north facing windows gave her the iridescence of a pop star rising out of artificial smoke. The main difference from any pop star that Susan had ever seen was the baby capsule that swung in the limp hand, brushing the high motorcycle boots.

Susan moved her head to follow the progress of the mother and child. There was no doubt in her mind as to the relationship. There was a slight dampness on the front of the T-shirt below the torn United States flag that formed a part of the group of symbols that Susan assumed was a gang badge. Then she had noted a suggestion of a safety pin behind the undone stud at the waist of the hand-mended leathers, though she could not imagine how the pin could have been anchored.

The most compelling sign as the girl and her burden came to rest was the hand that then felt the small body, and the fierce glare that was shot first at the capsule, and then at the slightly appalled face of a woman turning from the next register with a laden tray.

The duty manager glared over the counter and the mother took out a handful of small change and turned it over with selective care. The result did not seem to amount to much but she managed a cup of coffee and a miniscule bag of fries. Susan remembered the ravenous appetite of new motherhood and sympathised. She moved her seat so that she could follow the progress of this unusual madonna to a seat at a still uncleared table. Then she was distracted by a rush of children to the aquarium-like glass case of tumbling balls and bodies that stood in the centre of the shop. When she looked at the girl again she was talking to the woman at the next table. The blue suited lady handed over a silvery propelling pencil.

The startling surge of the tall figure to the door rivetted the attention of most people in her path. As she swept past Susan's table a folded page ripped from the courtesy copy of the daily paper could be glimpsed stuffed in the capsule, and there were pencilled rings round some of the blocks. The rest of the newspaper was strewn over the abandoned table.

The blue woman stood up and snatched her pen from the empty polystyrene cup and wiped the point ostentatiously on a paper napkin before tapping her way briskly through the same door. She paused outside and glanced carefully each way before starting confidently towards the big shop over the road. Susan moved more slowly. She saw in the distance that a capsule was propping open the door of a phone booth with a couple of people standing about outside with expressions of dissatisfaction.

Susan sat at the table in the kitchen that her mother and father had installed in the sixties. She had a sense of guilt and of slight physical discomfort, both the result of her indulgence at McDonalds. She sat in her old brown fuzzy jumper and woollen slippers and looked at the two men. For a moment she thought of the three of them as inhabitants of a small lair where they felt safe from the outside world. This was the place that the demands of others could be deflected by her ineffectiveness.

Theo – she thought – was hiding from his own sense of being out of place. He perched on the stool at the orange bench. He resembled a little grey tree-dwelling marsupial sitting there, with his claws round a glass and his legs hooked around the wrought iron legs of the stool. Grey hair was plastered across his broad balding scalp and little tufts sticking out behind his big ears showed that he had not budgeted for a haircut. It was strange that the effect was still so exotic and that the foreignness was so obvious. She assumed that behind the slightly protuberant eyes and pursed lips he was absorbed in a fantasy connected with the enormous pile of magazines she avoided scanning when she cleaned his room. Below him, squatting on a kitchen chair was her husband. His furry hands were clasped around the first tinny of the day, and there was a gleam in his normally inexpressive face. She wondered if he had won something on the dogs. The bib and brace outlined the bulge of his stomach and hips and for some reason she was suddenly full of tenderness. There was an assumed dependence on her in him. Fred needed a safe place as much as she did. Theo was both an intruder and a saviour.

The newspaper lay on the table. Fred looked at Theo and there was a strange sense of conspiracy between them. Susan resented the money spent on papers and was longing to say something. The only thing that restrained her was the memory that a small slice of housekeeping had been spent at McDonalds. Then she was glad she had been silent. She was afraid of Theo and his withering scorn of her Ocker ignorance. The fact that his board bridged the chasm that came before the end of each pension period made it worth all that, and she also sensed Fred's need for some excitement that Theo's exiled bitterness could provide.

Curry slopped from the ladle onto Fred's plate and he shovelled with gusto. More slowly the other two picked up their own plates, already spread with the contents of the microwave, and sat down. Susan wondered what the house would have been like without Fred. Certainly there would be no smell of curry. That was the relic of an army posting in some Asian country but she could not remember which. All those Slope countries sounded the same her father used to say.

The door resounded and Susan pictured the little scarred chrome knocker hitting home.

The smell of curry enveloped her as she opened the door. She played with the idea of buying a stronger air freshener. The setting sun had irradiated the pane of frosted glass giving a looming quality to the figure outside. Earrings were the first things Susan noticed. Lots of earrings at the level of the top of her own head. The right ear was studded like an old leather cinema seat seam glowing brassily in a row. The left was a whipped blanket edge with a binding of gold sleepers punching the lobe. The capsule was nowhere to be seen but in her hand the girl dangled a black full face helmet.

Blankly Susan heard that deep voice say,

"That room you advertised still free?"

Susan had an inexplicable thought that this was a creature of another species that spoke a language that did not bridge the gap. The big hand, still covered in a black glove, pushed forward the page from the classified section of the daily paper. With dislocation the shorter woman read the marked square, and then thinking she was mistaken she read its message again out loud, "Room suitable for mother and child". There was a phone number that duplicated the green dial on the black and glass table in the dark hall.

"An' the man on the phone said to come at once!" The apparition was slowly moving through the door and Susan slowly was having an impression that she had ceased to register on the visitor's global view.

The kitchen table was between the two men and the intruder. She sat down in the chair Susan had left pushed out and said, "About the room and me havin' a baby?" She had a little twist to her lips and looked at all three of them as if there was something unpleasant about to happen.

Fred pushed the casserole dish of curry towards her and followed up by shouting at Susan to get a fork and plate. The face below the spiky hair went a shade of grey and there was a suspicion of saliva on the full lips. Across the table the older man watched consideringly. For a moment she forked eagerly and then spluttered and choked. Susan forgot her discomfort, and spontaneously drew a glass of water from the slightly dripping tap. The girl swallowed it and looked at the plate with frustration. Susan lost the last vestiges of resentment. She pushed her as yet untouched 'Snitchel with Oven Fried Chips' over the table. After her surreptitious visit to McDonalds she was not hungry and at the back of her mind she knew she could always fill up before she slid into her side of the enormous sagging innerspring bed that had belonged to her parents. The girl wolfed. The grey man watched, then spoke.

"Do you have the bond and rent?"

Susan turned from filling the kettle. "Really, are you moving out?" She was surprised at the pleased tone of her own voice. Like the bed the house was part of her life, but somehow less her domain since Theo had been there.

Theo looked at her and shook his head. "So, the cot won't be used again and the sleep-out is empty."

She stared at Fred as that sentence penetrated. As the thoughts and implications came to the surface, her temples felt as if they were caught in a press and she could hear her voice say softly, "That was my baby's cot."

The next thing she saw was a small fan of grubby fifty dollar notes being displayed and then tucked again into a straining pocket.

She assumed the matter was settled, as the two men had stood up and the girl preceded them through the back door. She sat at the table and wondered why she did not leave. Fear of being alone welled through the anger. This was her sanctuary and always had been. She remembered her mother standing irresolutely by the front door and felt a strong identification with that shadowy woman.

Leaving the dishes on the table Susan wandered towards the fibro and corrugated iron shack behind the back verandah. While she had been out someone had piled a number of articles against the partly fallen palings of the fence. There was an old bike and the shopping trolley her mother had used for the last part of her life, as much as a support as a container. The men could be seen through the door facing someone out of sight. Theo's precise English carried through the still dusk.

"The cot and the bed are here now and you can have the rest of the baby things when you have more money."

For a moment she paused and the doorway filled the whole of her world. Measuring her distance, she turned to be out of sight when they came down the sagging step. Washing the dishes was her refuge. The men did not interrupt her, but Fred reached round her to get three glasses and a bottle of beer. There was a clang and the girl froze as the padded chair-back broke free of the chrome frame and hit the floor. Surprisingly Fred laughed.

"That's the problem with being big, love! Then look at me – big is beautiful!"

There was an answering glimmer from Theo.

Susan went on washing up. Water sprayed over her rings and through her fingers. For a moment the dishes became a small warm body and then the moment was gone. The capsule! She walked out of the front door and turned to the right. The raked shape of the bike was between the Kingswood and the slightly slimy fish buckets. Startled she wondered how the capsule had been secured as it now rested on the petrol tank, looped with a couple of loose straps. Susan picked it up and carried it to the kitchen. She unstrapped the child. Only then did the girl smile. She relaxed and put down her amber glass.

The men froze slightly. The baby mouthed at the protruding nipple and then the breast came free of the T-shirt and a light sucking filled the silence.

Susan fixed her gaze on the moving mouth and in her own flesh sensed when the baby released its grip and was turned in to face the other full breast. At the end of the feed the large hands turned the little bundle in her palms and were seen to rub and knead. There was a small coughing noise, and Susan passed a paper napkin over the table. The planes of the face that was framed by that extraordinary hair had changed and somehow softened. The mother picked up the empty capsule and with the baby drooping over her other arm like a much loved stuffed toy walked out of the room. Susan followed.

The most perfect bed in the world Susan had thought it when she was a child. But now it looked ridiculous. The mother leant her back against the headboard and the soles of her boots were pressed against the white foot. She watched Susan approach and lifted the bundle to be taken by the older woman. There was a little snuffle and a lurch like a cub in a litter, and then the small body relaxed at the soft crooning over its head. Susan sat on the edge of her bed with assurance and an air of belonging.

"Would you like a cuddle? There's something I have to do." The girl seemed both relieved and abashed at Susan's quiet content.

She moved over to the door. On the chest of drawers stood the helmet but she ignored it. She strode out of the sleep-out with a suspicion of a bounce and then the kitchen door screeched and swung.

"Talking of Macbeth..." (1995)

There were three people sprawled against the wall of the passageway between the living room and the bathroom. They viewed the opposite wall through a constant screen of moving legs as person after person collected a tinny or stubby from the cache buried in ice in the mildewed bathtub.

The party droned in the background, almost drowned behind the thumping shudder of the cheap sound system. Every now and again a thunderous hammering on the front door would herald another surging voice, and another figure crashed his burden into the ever full cauldron.

Malcolm decided that the image was in keeping with what he thought they were discussing, but decided not to share his inspiration with his companions. He remembered little of the first part of the night. However he had a confused memory of his own voice saying, "Of course, if I were makin' a movie of Macbeth, it would be Australian, you know, land claims, and witches with dingos and that sorta thing." What a topic for this bikie party into which he had been dropped. He was a real ghost at the feast, that was how he felt. Pleased, he recognised that for once his spongelike memory had released the right words on the right occasion.

Now the girl was slumped away from him and was leaning on the shoulder of a silver studded jacket. Incongruously the jacket was saying something about the power of evil and the endurance of the old religion. To Malcolm it made no sense, and yet was extremely logical in the way that a dream is logical. The girl craned her scrawny neck so she could gaze into the face of the young man in the leather jacket. She thought about power, his power, the strength in his biceps and the power that his Harley gave him to move frighteningly and urgently from place to place. Triggered by the train of thought, though she could not grasp the connection, came a clutter of words.

"Fair is foul, and foul is fair.

Hover through the fog and filthy air."

She fuzzily knew the words belonged to an old woman, not to the brilliant maleness next to her.

She had got her ambition, and now suspected it was but a disguised version of the same old trap. Vaguely she pondered on flight. But the moon was full. The paddock around the house had recently been mown, and she would have to cover several hundred feet before she reached the scattered feathery gums at the creek. In the other direction the grazing stretched to the hill. There was no shelter there. She had wished too hard and her wishes had been granted.

"This small hand … ." She waved it vaguely in front of her. Malcolm saw the bikie put his roll-your-own into the girl's fingers. She drew clumsily. She tried the thought again.

"If I wash my hands with Arab soap …"

The girl stared in front of her. Behind the unblinking, unfocussed eyes she reviewed the English class of the previous day. The others had whistled and clapped right through that revolting movie. The teacher had said it was directed by that man – couldn't remember his name now – y'know that man whose wife Manson's chicks had cut. That little red-haired bitch-witch, standing beside the teachers' desk with a piece of chalk in her fingers, rabbiting on about power, pretending all the time not to notice the blokes in the class betting each other behind cupped hands that she was a lessie! Linda giggled at the memory.

The movie had been the same story as the books they had got from the class set, but the books had been harder to read, being a play with strange long words and numbers on the ends of the lines. It had been all about these old blokes in armour. There had only been one woman who counted. She vaguely remembered that in the movie this Lady-Macbeth-person was young, really young. In a picture in the book she had looked older. The movie-star girl made more sense to Linda, because at yesterday's lesson the teacher had made a big deal about how, at the time the play was written, ladies younger than the girls in the class she was talking to, were married off to old guys.

Stuart, as usual being the class smartarse, had squeaked,

"What if they didn't get their periods, Miss?"

And Miss had looked down her nose and pretended not to hear. Anyhow, while the hubbub reigned around the desks, Linda had leaned back in that silly orange plastic chair with the wobbly leg and thought about being Macbeth's wife.

That night after school she had walked up the dirt track from the bus stop hoping that Dunc the Unc had bought frozen pizza for her to cook. He sometimes liked a real roast with veg, and he got so aggro when it took a long time. She remembered that she had just turned sixteen and grown up ladies could have what they wanted. With a slight thrill up the back of her calves, she walked carefully, lifting her feet rather than scuffing her soles on the dusty road as she experimented with a slight sway of her denim-clad hips.

Swirling dust suddenly enveloped her. On each side she saw a chromed wheel, its tyre still spinning against the gravel. To her right a worn boot heeled against a crumbling corrugation.

"Ooh!"

Then she giggled shrilly. She knew that her mouth would be hanging down and her neck stretched forward. On his motorbike he had reminded her of that Macbeth bloke on his horse.

"The youth worker at the Church told my sister you had a birthday. We guess we'll have to help you celebrate. Reckon you would like a hand to get rid of the old man."

She had stared at him numbly. This demigod had never before spoken to her. In fact she had not even scored a catcall as she passed the group that stood, riders and girls together, before the bike shop in the main street of the town.

"Is this the one with the pad?" asked the other man. The word 'pad' sounded strangely artificial in his rounded city-type speech. Linda thought he sounded like the actors on the telly.

She had walked into the house alone. The two men had waited at the mailbox at the turnoff. The rest of the blokes must be shown where to turn in, she had been told.

Her uncle had been pouring tea out of the old pot into his Irish whisky mug, the one he called his stirrup cup. Beside him was a new face, a man wearing a tie, though it was pulled down and his collar gaped as if to allow more space for the beer that was pouring from the neck of a bottle in a shallow arc over his tongue.

"Hi, pet, meet Malcolm." The elderly voice quavered through her consciousness. She had never heard the phrase 'deja vu', but suddenly she felt herself stepping onto a preordained path.

The middle aged stranger had looked at Linda, had seen a painfully young and gawky face with eyes that fixed on him with something like horror. Suddenly he felt desperately out of place.

"Well, I'll stay not upon the order of me goin."

He actually put down the bottle, but before he could move to the door his new friend had pushed another into his hand.

"Malcolm – he says he knows about the law. He's going to see me right over this business of your dad leavin' you this house that your grandma should have willed to me. She promised, you know!"

Six hours later Malcolm was sitting on the floor while the party continued around him. Wryly he reflected that it was just as well that most trips to sus out cheap country properties did not end this way. Of all things, he was now discussing Shakespeare's views on motherhood with this half-witted girl and some long-winded bikie who seemed to be able to quote that dead faggot of a poet as if he had the book in his hand.

He fished into his memory to keep up his end of the conversation. He had now lit his second rolled fag, and was in the reflective part of the evening.

"That must be the saddest line in the world."

The party milled around them. She cradled her Bundy and Coke and squinted through her clotted mascara. "I haven't got the faintest idea what your fucking talking about love."

"Her baby must have died," Malcolm said solemnly.

She turned to the man on her other side. He rolled words off his tongue.

"I have given suck, and know

How tender 'tis to love the babe that milks me."

She started to shiver, suddenly nauseous at the thought of what might have been. For the first time she noticed that Dunc was no longer in the room. She wondered where he was. Malcolm touched her arm, feeling gooseflesh.

"The ghost at the feast!" he said again, pleased that he could remember the phrase so clearly. He gave an inebriated snigger. "We must have seen the same movie."

The girl tried to follow his line of thought.

"The BBC Macbeth was more authentic than Polanski's," said the bikie, as if delivering some part of a lecture.

Much less certainly she fielded those names that she thought were familiar.

"That poor man ... his wife killed ... all that blood ..."

Leather jacket grunted with amusement.

"What all my pretty chickens and their dam
At one fell swoop."

The word 'chickens' and the dawn-bright silver of the moonlit sky bathing the uncurtained window struck a sudden nerve.

"The chooks," she squealed, "They've got to be fed. M'uncle'll go crook if they aren't fed early." She once again looked round for the old man. "What have you done with my uncle," she howled.

Her face distorted as the last of her sixpack of mixed drinks hit home. It was at that time she understood clearly that she was trapped within a mirror world of horrors. The hill and the river bank drew nearer, and Linda swooped to fly through the centre pane of the sashed picture window.

Her hand dripped blood and a shard of glass fell to the floor. She was still inside the house. Her surround was full of looming evil, mainly clad in black leather. One or two of these demons had just placed black domes where their heads should have been. She looked past the bloody mess of her own hand to the lino beneath, and there, bedaubed with freshly trickling blood, was her uncle curled up like a rather arthritic monkey with his hand clasping an empty bottle of Bailey's Irish Cream. Aghast the girl wiped her throbbing hand across her T-shirt. It was at that moment that she was convinced truly that she was one with Lady Macbeth.

Behind her a man said, "No, she's not going to be much fun. Still not a bad booze up. Let's stay."

"I don't know about the order of our going," said the Shakespearean bikie, "But I for one am getting out of here."

The old man had woken and was whimpering slightly. "You big blokes wouldn't hurt an old digger, would you mate?"

The invaders ignored him. "Let's split."

The troop, elite in their youth and regalia, bumped over the farm track, skidding into a swerve after the cattle grid, and past the sagging gate. As they rode down the short main street of the town, the moon briefly silvered the outline of their helmets as if they were a raiding party withdrawing to some mythical stronghold.

Back at the shack Duncan looked at his visitor. The man had his arm around Linda who had stopped crying and looked like a sleepwalker.

"So, this house is yours, then," he was asking tenderly.

Dragons of Bass Strait (1998)

Facing towards Antarctica
Sorrento Back Beach, Victoria, Australia.
Australia Day (26 Jan) 1989.

The girl stood on a rock. She wondered what difference it would have made had she ever been able to speak

- If I could talk, what would I say?

- I stand on a rock, and I think.

- I, Lisa. I am without speech, and yet I hear and see it all around me.

- I write in my head, and sometimes the words come out on paper.

- Who reads them? Well, there will be a reader this year, The Teacher sitting under the rock at the top of the beach. She is wrapped up in a scarf thing, and is talking to the man beside her. I think I will go on drawing Sea Dragons in my mind.

- Sea Dragons guard Bass Strait and devour sailing ships. The early steam ships too. Sea Dragons are less powerful against the screws which beat under containers, but they snack on bathers and even the occasional Prime Minister.

- What would The Teacher think if she could read my mind? God help us! She would probably think I believed that stuff. Then why not? One can know that the world spun itself out of cosmic dust and spawned visible life forms, but still envelop that certainty within the realities of Genesis and Milton. But that thought is for the future.

- In that Ocean the icebergs are born, and somewhere under their pear shaped hulls Dragons spawn, whipping up the white capped waves with their beating tails, calling out to the albatross who hover over them, watching sardonically as technoman tries to position an infallible eye out in the endless heavens. Occasionally those pointed tails will upturn a ship or smaller craft.

The imaginary world in her head became more solid.

- I wonder if Dragons ever come into Port Philip Bay, swimming up the shipping channels to accommodate their hulking shapes. They might come to catch sharks. The sharks come to eat the seals, but the Dragons can swallow a White Pointer whole, and make nothing of it. They could be there and no one know. They fade against other realities, and even their turds are invisible.

- They are basically nervous beasts, scared of hurting the people they find near them, and protective of the future of humans and themselves, in the shadow of circling, equally invisible space arrivals.

Briefly she flirted with the idea of a link between sea dragons and invisible extraterrestrials but the thought was a bit contrived and she was conscious she had lost the magic of her own world.

-So long as dragons are invisible to people, they cannot hurt one other.

-A speaking person would say that is ironic.

-I can talk too, though only in my head. The words invent a reality.

The Teacher looked across to the sea. The girl – her name was Lisa – stood on a rock that overhangs a pool. At her feet was a bevy of kids, surfing and swimming under the eye of a lifeguard. She balanced on the knobby rock, swaying her body in the wind, her ears stoppered against the roar of moving air, her arms curved upward. Behind her was a noisy and impatient cluster of youths with younger brothers and sisters in tow.

The Teacher turned to her husband.

"You see that girl on the rock? Her name is Lisa."

The man grunted and picked up the conversational baton.

"You mean the one with all the kids behind her." He pointed to the pool, which was a natural bowl rimmed by corroding concrete to trap the retreating tides.

The Teacher said, "She looks – I know it sounds odd in someone like that – joyous! The wind must be howling up there. Look at how she's got her hands in her ears."

"They might be anywhere under all that hair," said the man. "She might be posing as a Greek vase."

"That is silly! Not with all those kids and littlies behind her." Humour was not The Teacher's strong point. Behind her glasses she felt secure. "Well," she tried an imperceptible laugh. "I could be a film star on holiday in this scarf."

"No bikini?" grinned her husband.

"The Teacher forced a wider smile, uneasily aware that there was a trace of fantasy behind her own attempt at humour. "Feeling better about coming all this way?" She thought it was time to change the subject.

"Disguised like that you could have sat on the banks of the Yarra River in the middle of Melbourne, and the whole school could have gone past without recognising you." He was starting to think about the nose-to-tail drive back on this Australia Day afternoon.

"Well," she said. "I didn't want students coming up and talking to me. It is my holiday too!"

"What about her?" said her husband, pointing at the figure who was monopolising the jumping off point on the rock.

"Bill, she doesn't count. That is Lisa. It's as if she's always going to be a kid. Anyway, she isn't paying attention to anything. I always feel as if she's looking through me as if I were just shaped out of old Gladwrap!" The man looked at her and said nothing.

"Isn't it incredible," she said, "that one could go all the way to Antarctica without touching land." And then, with an uncharacteristic flight of fancy, she grinned. "Of course, you and I would make a nice snack for sea monsters!"

"Only if they like their food with shingle and sand flies," grunted her husband drowsily.

Then The Teacher's voice sharpened. "I wish the person with Lisa would do something."

"Why don't you if you're so concerned?"

"Thank God, it's not my business – but those kids behind her are really fed up!"

Across the beach came a shout. "Lisa, jump now!"

- I, Lisa

- I can feel someone shouting to make me move.

- I think I really want to jump. Why not?

- I leap from the rock, and I pass through time before the splash. But, alien in earth-air, I cannot pass though space. It opens and envelops me, so that I expect to fly but crash into spraying hardness, and then the acceptance of the water. My limbs no longer weigh heavily. My world here is without gravity. Not a fish, but knowing the feelings of a fish.

The girl leapt, clumsily hitting the water, her arms and legs twitching limply as she submerged. The water closed over her head and she sunk stonefish-like to the sandy bottom. Eventually she simply rose to the top, as slowly and motionless as if she indeed were in her natural environment.

"Oh! She's gone. She's sunk. Oh, no, she's jumping up and down with the littlies." The Teacher thanked the Lord that she did not have to intervene as Lisa repeatedly jumped up and dunked herself, deliberately wallowing among the toddlers with their blown-up monsters.

"Yes, Love, I'm ready to go." The Teacher turned, picked up her towel and followed in her husband's wake.

The day before school was to begin, The Teacher walked through the Chinese exhibition at the Art Gallery on her way to a concert in the Great Hall. Unconsciously she thought about curly, whirly dragons. She wondered whether Lisa had understood any of the previous year's curriculum on Western and Oriental Medieval Culture. Suddenly she was aware that this association had not been spontaneous, but that Lisa was sitting on a bench just in the outer edge of The Teacher's line of sight. The girl had her back to a floodlit glass case, and seemed to have no awareness of her surroundings.

- Tomorrow school, but today me, Lisa, in the Art Gallery among the Chinese Dragons.

- I can remember the Chinese names. If one sits in class and forgets the silly things the other kids say, the words in Arabic, Chinese and Japanese script in the illustrations in the history text book come to life.

- Unbelievably fleets dispersed by the Kamikaze storm and the Muslim conquerors moving west are the frame (in place if not in time) for Marco Polo threading the rope into the Chinese and European consciousness.

- The Alien of the pre-space era.

- Romance of names spans the gap. Contact was porcelain thin, tough yet brittle, depending on care to survive whole, yet enduring in fragments under a heap of shit. Spaghetti and gunpowder, opium and gold.

- I heard the Viking and the Cantonese in my class laugh together that day when The Teacher dropped her book, but I was the Alien. I could not see why that was funny.

- I will think back and say to myself, "I went to the Gallery, saw the blue and white bowl in its glass case, and, having seen it, sat with my back to its enclosed back-lit brilliance, enjoying its shape."

- The Museum at the other end of town has jade horsemen, tiny and large in different sections. Once there was an exhibition of clay horsemen, older by far than the blue and white bowl, but again with that ancient placidity, so far from the grim activity that the text book showed in Europe, in the Middle Ages of the continent where my ancestors spawned.

The school buildings sprawled over an enormous mound flanked by playing fields and abutting a noisy shopping centre. Beyond that ran a grey road, and beyond that again several square miles of houses. The first day of the school term the students had swarmed through the gate and scattered themselves into the maze of waiting classrooms.

At the back of Room 15, Lisa sketched in her mind the opening paragraphs of a description of her school day. She thought about how she would have spoken about coming into that room. Somehow the speech-thought was more like a recital than a monologue, perhaps because Lisa saw language better than she heard it. As a result she read her musings as if from a screen.

- "The person that I am came through the creaking sliding door, the heavy timber reluctant under my hand as the worn wheels bumped along the oilless runners. I paused as eyes raised, pair by pair, from the identical books on each identical desk. Some eyes were blue in freckled faces, and some were blue in Mediterranean sockets, offset by hair a little darker than that of the blue-eyed, mouse-blonde girl who had been ash-blonde the previous week and next week might well be black-haired in an awful travesty of Disney's Snow White. The brown and black eyes were more general but less striking. Closing my own mind against this barrage, I felt my way to a seat, closely followed by Sue."

What Lisa had not included in her imagined speech was the fact that Sue was her classroom aide appointed by the Department of School Education, a plump, dark-haired woman in her thirties, sporting a smock-like dress, and a determinedly schoolish demeanour. Sue was so much part of the scene that the girl did not even think to make her appearance clearer to an imaginary audience.

"G'morning, ten-bee! So nice to be back!" The Teacher beamed toothily, aglow with professional enthusiasm. The class grew slightly quieter and faced the front. She thought it was not a bad group, though she had her doubts as to how she would cope with one student in particular.

Inevitably the class wit had to make a comment. "Didn't slip, slap and slop enough, Miss!" The pink skin facing them flushed even more.

"Only one day at Sorrento." She forced a smile. "I got a lot of work done in the holidays!"

She eyed the group slouched in the orange plastic chairs, their sniggers almost hidden. The girl in the corner seat at the back was giggling too. However she looked overwrought rather than amused. The Teacher felt an involuntary "Damn" surface in her mind as she noticed that there were fresh tooth marks on the heel of Lisa's hand.

"My God, She's started biting herself again. Bugger these bloody idealists putting people like that in a real school. Just as all those Greek and Italian kids had left, along came the Vietnamese, and I only just got used to them, and now all these smart kids from Hong Kong – and they all want to go to medical school, though they are in Remedial English – and of course their Maths is good! – Well, Autistics are supposed to be good at Maths ..."

"Most of you know me," she said. "But in case you've forgotten!" She turned to the board and wrote, "Mrs. XXXX." She had expected them to be slightly amused, and she was also listening for the rustle and thump of paper and books being taken out. In her own mind she swore. "Shit!" She could not hear any laughs at her little witticism, but neither was there anything in the wriggling sounds behind her which sounded like the fat, hard covered text book she had waiting on the desk next to her briefcase.

"Is there anyone without a text?" she asked.

"Me, Miss!" chorused the class, putting up its collective hand.

"Put your hand up, Lisa," said a softer voice from the furthest corner. A small limp fist went up too, but it was propelled by a hand on the girl's elbow. The Teacher noticed that as usual the hand belonged to the plump older person sitting to her right.

When Sue had withdrawn her hand, the fist sank to half-mast in an awkward saggy pose, and stayed there.

"Put your hands down," said The Teacher. Lisa's fist stayed up.

"Why not?" said The Teacher, referring to the missing books.

A gabble arose. From the clamour she picked one voice.

"The stockists said they wouldn't be here till May!"

At the back of the class was a growling sound.

"Too much!" thought The Teacher. "No wonder those scars on her hands don't heal."

The students were shifting their buttocks deliberately on the roughened orange shells, more from boredom than anything else. With embarrassing enthusiasm the woman in the smock took up a pen and started taking notes. The Teacher blinked. She hadn't said anything that was of importance. Then she realised that the aide was writing a note to her charge.

The Teacher felt her world-weary teacher-eyes drift meaningfully around the echoing space filled with seated figures, though she found she could not bring herself to make real contact with the space around the teacher-aide and her companion. She picked up the chalk and turned to the board again. "The old remedy," she thought quickly.

"That is two pages." She underlined the words, and then wrote below, "Why I chose to study Geography this year."

"Remember, all work produced in class forms part of your folio for assessment!"

"Oh, no Miss!" Newly bleached blonde hair.

"Bimbo!" thought The Teacher, whose terms of abuse had been implanted at the same time as her attitude.

A typewriter appeared from somewhere under the hem of the aide's smock, and was pushed to the area in front of the non-speaking student so that she had to remove the clip-on lid herself and then roll a piece of paper onto the platen.

"This always fascinates me," thought The Teacher despite herself. For an instant she thought the speechless student would bite her hand again, because it hung in the air in front of her like a piece of meat. Then the aide raised her fingers and touched the girl on her forearm, and in that instant one could see the flaccid hand tighten slightly, and the forefinger separated from the rest of the digits. Then the wrist flexed slightly, well clear of the aide's palm. by now resting under the girl's forearm. The keys of the little battery-operated typewriter depressed in orderly sequence, and every few letters the determined forefinger stopped its prodding motion to rest on the space bar.

The Teacher walked up the aisles between the formica tables with their chipped edges and rough shredding chipboard, left behind as a decade of bored students had peeled off the rubber trim. From behind she could see what had already been printed in the first two lines.

"Geography and people are the opposing points of the place we occupy in the universe, and that is why this subject fascinates me."

The finger was swinging with more determination, and unexpectedly the aide grinned and said, "Don't be an ass, Liz. Try to think of something else!"

Lisa's mouth straightened into something which in another student would have been amusement, and she started again.

"Geography interests me because ..."

Halfway through the lesson The Teacher switched tasks.

"This squared paper," she said, handing out half a dozen sheets at the end of each row, "is like graph paper."

"Have a heart, Miss!" said the class clown, but copied down the scale for each axis without further protest.

"Not as difficult as it looks; just like a street directory, but this shows the height of the land."

The class drew contour lines, the coordinates plotted on the graph paper.

As every year, someone asked, "What happens if two lines touch?"

"A cliff," said The Teacher.

"... And where there is only one dot?"

"A peak!"

"But, Miss, the other lines near it are at sea level!"

"So, what do you think that minus sign means?"

The questioner sulked. "Mr. Brown said that if he taught us geography this year, we would do computer mapping."

"Not in my classroom!" said The Teacher, more vehemently than she realised.

"Mr. Brown thinks you're a Luddite!" The blond bimbo type looked up from her accurately drafted map and grinned.

"I must say something to that young man about not passing on staff room conversations to fifteen year old kids!" thought The Teacher.

"He was only joking about my hobby," she said disapprovingly. The class looked confused. She smiled briefly. "I weave," she said.

She imagined herself standing in the staff room and thundering, "Mr. Brown, how dare you be unprofessional enough to tell students you think my methods are out of date!"

Then, "I know I won't though," she thought sadly. She suddenly felt ineffectual and a little old.

At the back of the room Lisa's mouth emitted a small wailing croon of glee. The typewriter whirred, followed by the sound of paper being torn through, and the aide spoke sharply. "That's not very polite, Liz."

The Teacher pressed her forehead.

"Craig, either sit still or move to a desk which does not squeak."

"But I didn't do nuthin'!" he said.

The Teacher sighed to herself.

"Bloody no-hoper!" said The Teacher, but she said it to herself. She passed on, well aware that they understood each other.

The typewriter carriage printed out "b" then "five". Imperiously the girl pointed at the map.

"b5!" Sue spoke. "Is that your answer?" The finger pointed at "Y". The aide marked the spot. The Teacher leaned over.

"She still has the same problem as last year?"

"I'll show you," said Sue, and then, "You see, if I give her the pencil, even if I touch her, she can't draw the mark she told me to draw."

"Oh," said The Teacher. "Carry on then," and walked on.

"I suppose it is more important that she knows what to do, than doing it herself and getting it wrong," thought The Teacher, but the thought lacked conviction. She reached over the bimbo's shoulder, and could not quite keep the surprise out of her voice. "That's excellent, dear."

"I think you need to check your figures," she said to Craig.

"Contour lines again!" said The Teacher the next day. "How are you doing Lisa?" (Not expecting an answer).

"Finished already, dear? Not bad, Craig! Oh, fire drill!"

The Teacher noticed Lisa bite her hand and then block her ears as the whole class leapt to their feet simultaneously talking, laughing, pushing their chairs back with their bodies. They streamed out discussing what they would do over the weekend.

A tall boy with greasy hair pushed past.

"Hi, Liz!" he shouted, and moved on without waiting for an answer from the flushed face pressed into the mutilated hand.

"Liz, stop it. That hand looks terrible," from the Aide. "I've clipped the typewriter together, you carry it." The mouth on the hand said, "Arrr".

Deliberately, one move at a time, the girl stood up. As her plastic chair hit the ground she picked up her belongings from the desk clumsily and in no apparent order. When she had them all, she stepped away and turned to the door where The Teacher and the Aide were both waiting. As she walked between them, Lisa looked as if she were slightly nauseous as if the sudden change in pace had made her giddy.

- To move out of the classroom I have to push my chair back and stand up.

- It is strange that the other kids can talk and laugh and pick up books at the same time as they straighten their legs, so that their bums propel the plastic seat back on the timber floor. Then they rocket around, gossiping and planning what they will do over the long weekend.

- That is so weird – to be able to do all this in the same instant.

- No wonder they are unpredictable in all their actions.

- They seem to lurch through time, but with a fluidity which I do kind of envy but find terrifying.

- What would they make of my planet?

- There I stand, the gravity sensor in my skull working overtime to compensate for the variations in the hauling cords which invisibly bind me to its surface. That is why sometimes I sway against them. If they are not taut I might fall into the black hole of nothingness. Then sometimes they seem taut, but the anchorage points are frail. Those days I sit very still, my face frozen with fear as the slightest disturbance of these hawsers will tip the universe into oblivion.

"They are smoking, you know, behind the wattles on the oval." The staff room looked uninterested. "Lisa is over there too."

"Well, we don't have to worry about Lisa smoking. She gets her kicks out of rocking."

"That may be," said the P.E. teacher. "But she has no muscle tone. Real space child stuff!"

The staff moved on. "To get back to the question of the teacher on yard duty forgetting to check the end of the oval ...," said the Deputy Principal.

"We do!" said The Teacher. "But their lookout sees us a mile off."

"Not hard in her case," mumbled Mr. Brown, not quite quietly enough.

- Isn't it weird how adolescents are so territorial?

- On the train from our suburb to the city the private school girls have long, straight hair, or their hair has been cut in geometric precision. That is strange, because the girls at our local

High School have wild, shoulder length perms which are held together with scrunchies.

- Private School equals straight hair in this Year of Grace, but then how does one explain the witchlocks on the train from the city to the bay which top both private school uniform and ragged, wobbly, booby singlets from the local TAFE.

- Which do I wear? Why should I care what they say. Perhaps they say nothing, but in my mind they should.

- How can I be human if other humans do not expect me to be like them?

- Planet, galaxy, universe, anthill, menagerie. Why the train?

- There is a game I have seen some children play, called, I think, 'Pass the Parcel'. I really can't see the point, because after all that effort lots of people are disappointed when they have to unwrap it and, unbelievably don't get a prize.

- I gather that the fun essentially comes from the repeated experience of slight, predictable, disappointed screams in one's own head. They wouldn't put it like that! They would talk about what fun it is to gamble, even though they expect to lose. What the point of this is, I don't see.

- The human adolescent is like a Pass the Parcel player. Each great experience is just a repetition of the last, until something really odd happens. The last wrapping is removed, and Lo and Behold, one realises that is what adolescence was all about – pretending that things were important until like can start again

- Really the final wrapping is not specific to a certain age. Sometimes it is found almost as soon as childhood fades, and sometimes in middle age.

On her way home to cook dinner, The Teacher stood at the check-out

"I can't believe I never noticed before that the lollies are wrapped in a way that makes one want to touch them," she said to the girl on the till.

"Yes," said the cashier. "And they put them just where kids can reach them!"

While she rang up The Teacher's purchases, the latter continued the same train of thought. "I suppose kids over six have grown out of that. Thank goodness I moved into Secondary Schools. Small children are so demanding and impatient. Research would have been nice ..." she sighed. "Lucky Bill! No, of course we couldn't have had the babies if we had both ..."

Her own voice cut into her thoughts.

"Hoy!: She turned. "Where do you think you are taking that Mars Bar?" Her voice had the slightly infantile tone of someone who thinks she is speaking to a young child, and, by implication, to its mother. Then her gaze lifted and lengthened. "Lisa!" Her roar reached out across the space between where she stood, and where a solid stomping gingham dress was moving out of the shop.

A long-legged youth, who had moved into the gap at the check-out left by the girl, looked amused.

"Weird, isn't it Miss! She's so bright, and yet she still can't stop that!"

The Teacher looked more closely.

"I'm Craig in your geography class," said the youth, who, out of uniform and in torn jeans and a baseball cap, was quite indistinguishable from millions of teenage male animals all over the globe.

The Teacher glowered with embarrassment and affront.

"She's much better than she was last year," said Craig, and picked up her laden plastic bag to put it in the trolley for her, so that she had no alternative but to smile and thank him.

"Oh, I think she'll go home now," he continued in answer to her unspoken question. "She doesn't really have anywhere else to go."

"I'm sorry to worry you." The Teacher's voice echoed in the empty offices, the supermarket bag dragging her shoulder down.

"Really?" The Deputy-Principal looked up, his voice sceptical.

"I thought you would like to know about this." Her voice droned on.

"Thank you," he said, not leaving his desk until she had cleared the building. He then spoke into the phone. "Hello. I'm glad I caught you. We have a little problem here ..."

- I wade into the sea. The waves at my ankles. The waves at my knees. I am still Lisa, but I am not Lisa-at-School.

- The dragons are there. They frolic and breach, their scales mother-of-pearl in the sunlight, jewelled with droplets of salty water. They wait for me and for my friends.

- I can hear shouts and see people with caps running into the sea. Now they are pointing far off, towards the waveless spread beyond the breakers. That helicopter – it's not sent out to see dragons, though it circles, then flies along the coast towards the Heads.

- To ride a dragon?

- Of course I ride dragons! That is what I was born for. The water's at my waist, my shoulders.

- Did the class talk about helicopters? Not that I remember. Perhaps they think metal dragonflies are more real than dragons. I should have thought to type – to ask – last time I sat at a table.

- They will be there tomorrow with their books, their pens, their voices. Their laughter comes with me. The water to my ears. Mixed with the kids' laughter is dragon laughter.

- I feel the strength of the dragon's tail, the roughness of the skin of its back as I am dashed below the water. I am happy.

- I ride the dragon.

"Everyone here?" The Teacher wrote Monday's date on the board.

"They're not!" said the bimbo, shrugging her shoulder in the direction of two empty seats in the back row.

"Oh?" said The Teacher.

"Did you go to Sorrento yesterday, Miss?" asked Craig. "There was a drowning there, wasn't there?"

"I think a man got out of his depth and was swept out to sea. They haven't released a name yet, have they?"

"No," said Craig, who fancied himself as a surfie. "I think they will have to retrieve the body. Apparently no one's been reported missing. That rip could swallow the Olympic swimming team, and they wouldn't have a chance."

"What a way to go," said the bimbo. "Nothing between the Sphinx rock and Antarctica."

"There might be dragons!" said an anonymous voice on the right.

"I don't think this is a topic for joking!" said The Teacher.

"Chomp, chomp!" A subversive mutter.

"Hey," said a girl's voice. "That's strange!"

The Teacher felt a slight thrill of premonition.

"What?" she barked. "What now?"

"There's a scrap of typing paper on this table."

"Put it in the bin!"

"Don't you want to know what she said?"

"No!" snarled The Teacher.

The class disregarded her.

"Read it, read it," they chanted.

The girl obediently dropped it in the bin, where it lay face up in the empty liner.

"It was torn, but I think it said something about a dragon."

"What a coincidence!" said The Teacher. "Now could you get on with your work.?

The Delphi Connection: a fragment (1995)

The bay was small, just a little arm of the sea. To the west a little cape cut it off from the Gulf of Corinth, and formed a rock face on which the rays of the just-rising sun drew a dark line where a ledge ran steeply from the headland to the rough broken pebbles at the end of the inlet. On the side opposite the cliff, the sea had deposited a small shelly beach. The tide had dropped so there was room for half a dozen or so people who stood, shivering slightly, their backs to the dawn sky.

Only one was a woman. Although she appeared nearer her fortieth than thirtieth year she was slim, her waist not thickened by frequent childbearing. She was richly dressed as if a just-maturing girl awaiting a kingly bridegroom, but incongruously, her hair was arranged in the style of a married woman of the city of Thebes. Beside her was a youth, gloriously decked out in bronze battle gear. His helmet was held by a body slave.

A little removed was a cluster of three older men, as if there as witnesses. The whole party seemed to have travelled some distance, the older men's well-made sandals were thick with dust, and just above the beach was a chariot, its horse chomping at the sparse seaside grass.

The watchers gazed resentfully across the water, their heads tilted back. Above the sloping ledge which in happier times formed part of the well-trodden pilgrim route from Thebes to Delphi, an enormous flat rock had come to rest, its bulk overhanging the path like an incomplete arch. On this natural

51

dais rested an extraordinarily beautiful figure, her massive forepaws dangling negligently over the edge, her wings still black against the dispersing grey of early morning and the rays of the sun irradiating the surface hairs of her wonderfully tawny coat. As with all sphinxes, only her face was human. It frowned slightly. All her attention was on the point where the road from Delphi came into view.

It was an unusually large Sphinx, thought Creon, hitching at the strap which held his breastplate. The temporary ruler of Thebes was surprised to realise that he was suddenly more irritated than terrified by the Sphinx. The irritation was also combined with a slight suspicion he might appear a little ridiculous as the breastplate had belonged to his late brother-in-law, and was just a little large.

However he supposed he should be grateful that the enormous band of robbers who had banged the late King Laius over the head, and slaughtered all but one of his attendants (who had returned with the injuries to prove his own bravery), had for some mysterious reason left all his valuables, including his armour, untouched. Thebes was hardly in a position to commission a new set of armour for its new warlord – that is if they were lucky enough to get one smarter than a cat.

The drought had caused enough financial problems, which was why Laius had gone off incognito to bother the Oracle. One would have thought, continued the brother of Laius' widow, that, after his last encounter with Apollo just after his marriage that the old man would have left well alone.

Now there was this damned Sphinx, rampaging up and down the roads to north and south, asking unanswerable riddles of travellers, flying back to this spot with them wriggling in her claws, and then guzzling them down, jewels, cash and all. This seemed an appalling waste to Creon, as travellers tended to relax in the taverns of Thebes, and after a few cups of wine were more than happy to lose heavily in games of chance with an aristocratic young gambler.

The merchants had begun complaining too about the falloff in trade and refusing to pay their taxes. It had become so bad that he had happily agreed with the elders to let the word be spread throughout Greece that the wife and throne of King Laius would be bestowed on whoever defeated the monster. However the way things were going now, he might be stuck with this boring kingship business for ever. Of course he had no objection to being royal, but as Regent there was a lot too much hanging around appearing dignified to suit him. Taverns were temporarily off limits.

He touched the woman on the shoulder, smiling at her in what he hoped was an encouraging way.

"Don't worry, Jocasta, we'll have a new man in your bed any day now!"

It was strange, he thought to himself, but she had not seemed at all grieved by Laius' death. If anything she was relieved, and less than concerned that his remains be properly retrieved and buried here in the place where he belonged, so that the soul, escaping as if a butterfly, might remain free but safe near its own body. All she said was, "Never speak of Laius again in my presence!"

And when he had later told her of his decision about her future marriage, she had replied in a most unseemly manner as if she had rights in the matter.

"Little brother!" She had shrugged her shoulders and laughed. "I make a condition." and before he could say what was on the tip of his tongue she had continued, "As long as he never, like the others around me, speaks of or even hears of Laius. He who dies without sons, let his name die too.

Remembering the viciousness in her voice, Creon wondered if she would do what he hoped would be required of her.

Jocasta shifted under his gaze, and continued her own line of thought.

"Laius, that old goat. He took me for the children I would bear him, killed the one I did bear and, as punishment for an even older offence, lived in fear of fathering his own child for the rest of his days!" She started to giggle as if she had been told a joke at a woman's feast.

Creon glared at her. Really the woman was becoming odder and odder. The old men behind shifted in their swathed cloaks and pretended to hear nothing. Jocasta could have been heard to murmur sardonically, "Man's business! Men's business I was ..." Her voice trailed off as her brother jabbed her in her ribs.

Internally she continued, "And men's business I am again, although Creon is hardly a man. A crying child when I became queen and flowed with the blood and fluid of my own child's birth. Laius the Damned! He sinned but why was I ... ? I bore my babe and lost it from my own arms. I could not save it, but at least I tore it swaddled and screaming from the murderer so he did not hurt it any more. The shepherd took you, you had no burial, no rebirth."

Her nose began to run and she sniffed, wiping her hand across her face like a peasant girl. At a gesture from his master the slave offered her a cloth. Jocasta buried her face in its soft white folds. In her mind she stood near her father's hearth, a fourteen-year-old bride-to-be. Her mother's arms held her safe. The great soft furred housedog leaned against Jocasta's thighs, breathing heavily so that the vibrating ribs made her one with his warmth.

The memory was so real that when she lifted her head and opened her eyes she was shocked to find herself across the shimmering strip of water, barely milky in the new daylight. From the distance came what might have been a friendly snarl, or even a giant purr. The men looked on, faintly shocked. The two women might as well have spoken.

Jocasta looked up at the slaveman who was waiting to retrieve the white cloth. Her astonished whisper lay on the dawn air.

"I am promised – that she swears – that none of my children, whether born before now or yet to come, will lack full funeral rites."

The slave looked, expressionless, at her radiant face. Yet again the three older men politely tried to notice nothing.

Creon sighed. If the hand of Jocasta and the kingship of Thebes were to lure someone able to confound this monster, it looked as if it had better be soon before she collapsed into complete insanity. Then abruptly he lost all interest in his sister's peculiarities.

For an instant the sun blazed more fiercely than he could remember in his whole life. Around the great human-yet-feline throat, above the golden furred shoulders, a mirrored pendant of the kind sacred to Apollo changed from a sheen of gold to reflect sparking-blue arrowed light. A blade of time sliced the great purr.

On her clawtips the Sphinx arched, her fur standing fanlike along her spine. Her wings flapped, not as if she were soaring, but in terror against some unseen assailant. Jocasta moved a step forward, as if to comfort a friend.

Then, as suddenly as she had changed, the Sphinx was her usual self, sitting on her rock. She faced the east, gazing appealingly over the heads of her mystified audience and into the rising sun.

So she did not immediately notice the foreigner, a Corinthian by his dress, who seemed to amble into sight from the direction of Delphi. Creon expected him to turn back when he saw the Sphinx, but the young man continued his slow way, his face shaded by a broadbrimmed hat.

Now the watchers saw that he limped as if from birth, his whole body, supported on a clublike staff, rocking slowly as his feet turned, one thicker than the other but both twisted and swollen.

The Sphinx seemed to have finished her rapt silent plea. She stretched and yawned, turning to face the traveller.

"Oedipus," The men heard her speak for the first time. "What do you want?"

The man seemed startled, but in some strange way not surprised. His long cloak had rusty stains on it as if he had been bloodied in some long-gone battle. Now he looked at the Sphinx with weary interest. She was probably the first living thing he had seen for days in that deserted countryside.

He approached nearer, stopping just out of claw's reach.

The conversation was inaudible to the Thebans, but a decade later Creon realised it must have gone something like this.

"I am puzzled, Sphinx."

The tide had started to run and little waves were sucking and splashing at the rocks below so Oedipus drew nearer in case she did not catch what he was saying. He recoiled slightly as her enormous human head swung towards him, noted that she seemed herself to be slightly gaunt, and also that her slitted human eyes were enhanced by the suggestion of a third lid. He persevered, no doubt because, in spite of their sinister nature, sphinxes also have a reputation for wisdom.

"Madam Sphinx."

"Urrr."

"I have a puzzle for you."

Silence from the great furred chest.

"Madam Sphinx, on the road from Delphi some time back, I met five ageing men."

Still no sound and he swallowed self-consciously but continued.

"One attendant I struck when his master in the carriage bade him not to give way to me. I think he died of shock, because when I later tried to rouse him, his face was twisted and he had an expression of fear."

The head inclined once.

"The old man in the carriage meantime slashed at me, and I dealt him a blow on the temple that killed him. The horses in their harness were spirited and strong. They panicked, their flying hooves striking and the wooden wheels killing two of the others. One only, a herdsman by dress, who I suppose was there to care for the animals, survived – or I suppose did if the wolves did not get him, for he ran to the hills. Sphinx, counsel me. I am no warrior, what should I do to expunge any blood guilt?"

He peered from under the brim of his hat, his face contorting as he caught the foetid cat breath from her all too human mouth. The Sphinx seemed amused. The sea was smooth for a moment as the wind shifted. The Sphinx's voice could be heard again.

"Around here, little man, I ask the riddles."

Her golden flanks were now iridescent in the strengthening sunlight. To Creon's amazement they quivered as if reflecting the giggle that had earlier overwhelmed his sister.

"However, hear me well. It is the will of my master, the Lord Apollo, these things remain secret until the time appointed by fate."

The traveller bowed his head.

"And now," purred the Sphinx, "It's riddling time."

The little mound of torn and shattered bones below her was being scanned by the first gulls of the day, no doubt as a prelude to better things to come. The wind ruffled the waters again, so that the Thebans could only catch fragments of her voice.

"... morning ... four legs ... ... noon ... legs ... ... the night ... three?"

Astonishingly the stranger laughed. He tossed his club spear-like a full ten paces. It sailed past the point where the path ran under the projecting tip of the Sphinx's crag. It came to rest, handle uppermost, projecting from a stiff, round bush. Then he pulled off his cloak and hat, moving closer but still out of reach of a paw which was poised scythe-like in the air.

Suddenly he flung his burden away, the hat cartwheeling on the wind, and his rusty cloak flapping across the beautiful face. The Sphinx blinked.

At that moment Oedipus dropped to his knees and scuttled on all fours under the overhang. A huge paw fished just behind his fleeting legs. As the Sphinx rose to stretch her wings for the swoop, he rose to his feet and frantically hobbled a couple of paces to the bush where his stick was held. He grabbed it and leant on it just in time to avoid collapsing into the dust. His voice screamed triumphantly above the rising waves.

"Oh Sphinx, like me, a man!"

From that moment the lame man behaved as if the Sphinx had already ceased to exist. He walked back and retrieved his hat and cloak, wrapping the latter around his body, but holding the hat in his hand. So he was bareheaded when he moved down the last curves of the rocky path.

He ignored the advancing chorus of men. He looked beyond them and put out his hand, dropping his hat into the sand.

"I am come home," he said, though he did not know what he meant by saying it.

Above the inlet the Sphinx shuddered, her wings pressed close to her side. Apollo's medallion again flared.

As if cast in stone she fell to the sea, spearing the water to disappear in a myriad of multi-coloured droplets that might have been crystal butterflies.

About the Author

Lucy Blackman was born in Melbourne, Australia. Between 1987 and 1993, the years in which several of these stories are set, she divided her time between the Mornington Peninsula which backs onto the Great Southern Ocean, and the city suburbs. Lucy now lives in Brisbane, Queensland.

Read more at www.lucysautismstory.com.